CONTE[NTS]

1	The Meeting of the Four Cousins	5
2	The Old Cottage on the Hillside	12
3	A Chapter of Quarrels	23
4	A Walk and a Surprise	35
5	A Rescue and a Strange Discovery	44
6	A Disappointment – and a Picnic	52
7	Miss Mitchell is Very Cross	64
8	Down the Pot-hole	72
9	In the Heart of the Mountain	81
10	A Very Strange Discovery	88
11	The Hunt for the Two Spies	96
12	The End of the Adventure	105

Enid Blyton titles available at Bloomsbury
Children's Books

Adventure!
Mischief at St Rollo's
The Secret of Cliff Castle
Smuggler Ben
The Boy Who Wanted a Dog
The Adventure of the Secret Necklace

Happy Days!
The Adventures of Mr Pink-Whistle
Run-About's Holiday
Bimbo and Topsy
Hello Mr Twiddle
Shuffle the Shoemaker
Mr Meddle's Mischief
Snowball the Pony
The Adventures of Binkle and Flip

Enid Blyton Age-Ranged Story Collections
Best Stories for Five-Year-Olds
Best Stories for Six-Year-Olds
Best Stories for Seven-Year-Olds
Best Stories for Eight-Year-Olds

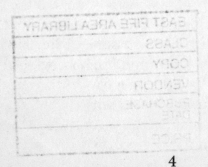

CHAPTER 1

THE MEETING OF THE FOUR COUSINS

Two children and a dog raced down to the village sweet-shop in excitement. They opened the little door of Mrs MacPherson's shop and went inside.

'Good morning,' said Mrs MacPherson, in her soft Scottish voice. 'You looked excited, the two of you.'

'We are,' said Sandy, a tall boy with a jolly, freckled face. 'We've got our English cousins coming to live with us till the war's over! We've never even seen them!'

'They're about the same age as we are,' said Jeanie, Sandy's sister. 'One's called Tom, and the other's called Sheila. They live in London, but their parents want them to go somewhere safe till the war's over. They're coming tomorrow!'

'So we've come down to get some of your bull's-eye peppermints for them,' said Sandy.

'And will they do lessons with Miss Mitchell your governess?' asked Mrs MacPherson, getting down her big jar of peppermint humbugs. 'It will be right nice company for you.'

'It's to be hoped the town children don't find it dull down here,' said Mrs MacPherson, handing over a fat bag of sweets. Sandy and Jeanie stared at her in surprise.

'*Dull!*' said Jeanie, quite crossly. 'How could anyone find Kidillin dull? There's the river that rushes through Kidillin, and the hills around, and away yonder the sea!'

'Ay, but there's no cinema for twelve miles, and only three shops, not a train for ten miles, and no buses!' said Mrs MacPherson. 'And what will town children do without those, I should like to know?'

The two children left the little shop. They gazed into the two other ships of Kidillin – which were general stores, and sold most things – and then made their way home again, each sucking a peppermint.

Sandy and Jeanie were really indignant at the thought that anyone could be bored with Kidillin. They loved their quiet Scottish life, they loved Kidillin House, their home, and enjoyed their lessons with Miss Mitchell, their old governess. They knew every inch of the hills about their home, they knew the flowers that grew there, the birds and the animals that lived there, and every cottager within miles.

Sandy and Jeanie were to drive to the nearest town to meet their cousins the next day. So, with Miss Mitchell driving the horse, they set off. It was a long way, but the autumn day was bright and sunny, and the mountains that rose up around were beautiful. The children sang as they went, and the clip-clop of the horse's feet was a pleasant sound to hear.

The train came in as they arrived at the station. Sandy and Jeanie almost fell out of the trap as they heard its whistle. They rushed through the little gate and on to the platform.

And there stood a boy and girl, with a pile of luggage around them – and a dog on a lead!

'Hello!' cried Sandy. 'Are you Tom and Sheila?'

'Yes,' said the boy. 'I suppose you are Sandy and Jeanie? This is our dog, Paddy. We hope you don't mind us bringing him – but we couldn't, we really *couldn't* leave him behind!'

'Well, I hope he gets on all right with *our* dog,' said Sandy doubtfully. 'Mack is rather a jealous sort of dog. Come on. We've got the trap outside. The porter will bring out your luggage.'

The four children, the dog, and a porter, went out to Miss Mitchell. She shook hands with Tom and Sheila, thought that Sheila was very pretty,

but far too pale, and that Tom was too tall for his age. But they had nice manners, and she liked the look of them.

'Welcome to Scotland, my new pupils!' said Miss Mitchell. 'Get in – dear me, is that your dog? I hope he won't fight Mack.'

It looked very much as if Paddy would certainly fight Mack! The two dogs growled, bared their teeth and strained hard at their leads. Their hair rose on their necks and they looked most ferocious.

'What an unfriendly dog Mack is,' said Tom. This was not at all the right thing to say. Sandy looked angry.

'You mean, what an unfriendly dog your Paddy is,' he said. 'Our Mack would have been pleased enough to see him if he hadn't growled like that.'

'Mack can come up on the front seat with me,' said Miss Mitchell hastily. She didn't want the cousins to quarrel within the first five minutes of their meeting.

'Then I shall drive,' said Sandy at once. He wasn't going to sit behind in the trap and talk politely to a boy who was rude about Mack.

'Can you drive this trap yourself?' said Sheila in surprise.

'Of course,' said Sandy. 'I've driven it since I was four.' He thought Sheila was rather a nice girl – but Jeanie didn't! Jeanie thought Sheila was too dressed-up for anything!

'How does she think she's going to walk on the hills in *those* shoes?' thought Jeanie scornfully, looking at Sheila's pretty button-shoes. 'And what a fussy dress! All frills and ribbons! But I like Tom. He's nice and tall.'

They drove home. Miss Mitchell did most of the talking, and asked the two London children all about the home they had left. They answered politely, looking round at the countryside all the time.

'Doesn't it all look awfully big, Sheila,' said Tom. 'Look at those mountains! Oh – what a funny little village! What is it called?'

'It is Kidillin,' said Jeanie. 'We live not far away, at Kidillin House. Look – you can see it above those trees there.'

Sheila and Tom looked at the plain, rather ugly stone house set on the hillside. They did not like the look of it at all. When they had gone to stay with their uncle in the English country-side the year before, they had lived in a lovely old thatched cottage, cosy and friendly – but this old stone house looked so cold and stern.

'I hope the war will soon be over!' said Tom, who really meant that he hoped he wouldn't have to stay very long at Kidillin. Sandy and Jeanie knew quite well what he was really thinking, and they were hurt and angry.

'They are as unfriendly as their dog!' whispered Jeanie to Sandy, as they jumped down from the cart. 'I'm not going to like them a bit.'

'I wish we were at home!' whispered Sheila to Tom, as they went up the steps to the front door. 'It's going to be horrid, being here!'

CHAPTER 2

THE OLD COTTAGE
ON THE HILLSIDE

For the first few days things were very difficult for all four children, and for the two
dogs as well. They were even more difficult for
poor Miss Mitchell! Sandy and Jeanie never
quarrelled – but now she had four children who
bickered and squabbled all day long!

As for the dogs, they had to be kept well
apart, for they each seemed to wish to tear the
other to pieces! They had to take it in turns to be
tied up so that they could not fly at one another
all day long.

'And really, I'm wishing I could tie up the
children too,' Miss Mitchell said to Sandy's
mother. 'For they're like the dogs – just ready to
fly at one another's throats all day long!'

Mrs MacLaren laughed. 'Give them time to
settle down to each other,' she said. 'And you'd
better begin lessons again tomorrow, Miss

Mitchell – that will keep them out of mischief a bit.'

Sandy and Jeanie had been showing off to Tom and Sheila. They had taken them for a long walk, up a difficult mountain, where a good deal of rough climbing had to be done. The English children had panted and puffed, and poor Sheila's shoes were no use at all for such walking.

'Can't we have a rest again?' asked Sheila at last. 'I'm so tired. This is a dreadful place for walking. I'd much rather walk in the park!'

'In the *park*!' said Sandy scornfully. 'What, when there's fine country like this, and soft heather to your feet! And look at the view there – you can see the sea!'

The four children sat down. Far away they could see the blue glimmer of the sea, and could hear very faintly the shrill cry of the circling gulls. Tom was so tired that he only gave the view a moment's look, and then lay down on his back. 'Phew, I'm tired!' he said. 'I vote we go back.'

'But we're not yet at the burn we want to show you,' said Jeanie. Sheila giggled.

'It does sound so funny for a stream to be called a *burn*!' she said. 'It sounds as if something was on fire – going to see the *burn*!'

'The bur-r-r-rn, not the *burn*,' said Sandy, sounding the *R* in burn. 'Can't you talk properly?'

'We can talk just as well as *you*!' said Tom, vexed, and then off they went, squabbling again!

Mack, who was with the children, barked when he heard them quarrelling. He wanted someone to quarrel with too! But Paddy was at home, tied up, much to Tom's annoyance.

'Be quiet,' said Tom to Mack. 'I can't hear myself speak when you begin that noise. Where are you going, Sandy? I want to rest a bit more.'

'There'll be no time to finish the walk if you lie there any longer,' said Sandy. 'This is the fourth time we've stopped for you – a lazy lot of folk you Londoners must be!'

'All right. Then we'll *be* lazy!' said Tom angrily. 'You and Jeanie go on, and Sheila and I will stay here till you come back – and you can go and find your wonderful bur-r-r-r-rn yourself!'

'Oh do come, Tom,' begged Jeanie. 'It really is a strange sight to see. The water comes pouring out a hole in the hillside – just as if somebody had turned a tap on!'

'Well, don't you go rushing up the mountain so quickly then,' said Tom, getting up. 'I'm sure you're just showing off! I bet you and Jeanie don't go so fast when you're alone! You're just trying to make us feel silly.'

Jeanie went red. It was quite true – she and Sandy had planned together to take the two Londoners for a stiff walk up the mountains, going at a fast pace, just to show them what Scots children could do. And now Tom had guessed what she and Sandy had planned.

'Oh come on,' said Sandy impatiently. They all went up the steep, heathery slope, rounded a big crag, and then slipped and slid on a stony stretch that scratched Sheila's shoes to bits!

Suddenly there was a rumble of thunder round the mountain. Tom looked up anxiously. 'I say! Is there going to be a storm?' he said. 'Sheila always gets a cold if she gets soaked. Is there anywhere to shelter?'

'There's an old tumble-down hut not far from here,' said Sandy. 'Come on – run!'

The rain began to fall. The four children and the dog ran full-pelt over the heather – up another slope, round a group of wind-blown pine trees – and there, in front of them, tucked into the mountainside, was an old, tumble-down cottage!

The children rushed to the door, flung it open and ran inside. They shook themselves like dogs, and the rain flew off their clothes, just as it was flying off Mack's coat. Then Sandy gave a cry of surprise.

'I say! Somebody lives here! Look!'

The children looked around the little stone house. It was roughly furnished with chairs, a table and two camp beds. An oil-stove stood in a corner, and something was cooking on it.

'Funny!' said Jeanie, staring round. 'Nobody's here at all – and yet there's something cooking on the stove.'

'Perhaps there's someone in the tiny room at the back,' said Sandy, and he pushed open the door and looked inside. The boy stopped in the greatest surprise. Nobody was there – nobody at all – but the whole room seemed full of a strange-looking machine, that had knobs and handles, valves and levers on it. Sandy was just going to tell Tom to come and see, when he heard footsteps.

He shut the door of the little room quickly, just as the door of the house swung open, and a fat man came in. He was so astonished when he saw the children that he couldn't say a word. He stood and gaped at them in amazement. Then he turned a purple-red and caught Tom by the shoulder.

He made peculiar noises, and pushed the boy out of the door so roughly that he almost fell. He was just about to do the same to Jeanie when Sandy stepped up and stopped him. The boy stood there in his kilt, glowering at the angry man.

'Don't you dare touch my sister!' he said. 'What's up with you? There was a storm coming on, and we came in here out of the rain. We didn't know anyone lived here – it's always been empty before. We'll go if you don't want to give us shelter!'

There was the sound of footsteps again and another man came into the house, looking dismayed and astonished. He began to roar at the children.

'What are you doing here? Clear out! If you come here again I'll set my dog on you!'

The children stumbled out of the old hut in a fright. The second man caught hold of Tom and shook him. 'Did you go into the room at the back?' he demanded. 'Did you? Go on, answer me! If you've come to steal anything, you'll be sorry.'

'Of course we haven't come to steal anything!' said Tom indignantly. 'No, I didn't go into any room at all except the one you found us in – I didn't even know there *was* another room! So keep your silly secrets to yourself!'

The man made as if he would rush at him, but Mack somehow got in between, and tripped the man over. He sat up nursing his ankle, looking as black as thunder.

'Loose the dog, Carl!' he yelled. 'Loose the dog.'

'Come on,' said Sandy at once. 'It's a big brute of a dog. I can see it over there. It would eat Mack up!'

The four children flew down the path in the

rain. No dog came after them. The rain poured down, and Tom looked anxiously at Sheila again. 'We really shall have to shelter somewhere,' he said. 'Sheila is getting soaked and I promised Mother I'd look after her.'

'There's an overhanging rock by the burn we wanted to show you,' said Sandy stopping. 'But it's rather near that old hut. Still, the men won't see us there, and they'll think we've gone home frightened, anyway. Come on!'

Sandy led the way. In a few minutes they came within the sound of rushing water, and then Tom saw a great craggy rock. They went towards it, and were soon crouching under it out of the rain.

'This is the burn, or stream we wanted to show you,' said Sandy. 'Look – it gushes out of the hole in this rock – isn't it strange? It comes from the heart of the mountain – we always think it's very strange.'

It *was* strange. There was a large, uneven hole in one side of the great rock, and from it poured a clear stream of water that fell down the mountainside in a little gully it had made for itself. On and on it went down the mountain until, near the bottom, it joined the rushing River Spelter.

'Jeanie and I have climbed down beside this water all the way from this stone to the river,' said Sandy proudly. 'It's very difficult to do that. We had to take a rope with us to get down at some places, because the burn becomes a water-fall at times!'

Tom was very interested in the torrent that poured out of the hole in the rock. He went close up to it and peered into the hole, whose mouth was almost hidden by the spate of water.

'Does this water get less when there are no rains?' he asked. Sandy nodded. 'Yes,' he said, 'it's very full now, for we've had heavy rains the last week or two. Wouldn't it be exciting to crawl through that hole, when the water was less, and see where it led to!'

'Where does the River Spelter rise?' asked Tom. 'In this same mountain?'

'Nobody knows,' said Sandy. Tom looked astonished.

'But hasn't anyone followed it up to see?' he asked.

'No,' said Sandy with a laugh. 'It's like this burn here – it suddenly flows out of the mountain, and no one has ever dared to seek its source, for it would mean swimming against a strong current, in pitch black darkness, underwater! And who would care to do that!'

'How peculiar,' said Tom thoughtfully. 'This is a more exciting place than I thought – springs that gush out of rocks, and rivers that come from underground homes – and strange men that live in secret tumble-down huts!'

'Let's start home again now,' said Sandy, suddenly remembering the two men and their dog. 'It's stopped raining. Tom, remind me to tell you something when we get back.'

Down the mountain they went – and poor Sheila quickly decided that it was far worse to go down steep slopes than to go *up* them! She was tired out when at last they reached Kidillin House.

'Oh, Sandy, you shouldn't have taken Tom and Sheila so far,' said Miss Mitchell, when she saw Sheila's white, tired face. 'And look – the child's soaked through!'

Sandy and Jeanie were ashamed of themselves when they saw that Sheila really was too tired even to eat. They went to tie up Mack, and to let Paddy loose.

'Anyway, we've shown Tom and Sheila what sillies they are when it comes to walking and climbing!' said Sandy. 'Oh – where's Tom? I wanted to tell him something!'

He found Tom groaning as he took off his boots. 'My poor feet!' he said. 'You're a wretch, Sandy – you wait till I find something I can do better than you!'

'Tom,' said Sandy. 'Listen. I peeped inside the back room of that old tumble-down hut – and do you know, there was a whole lot of machinery there. I don't know what it was – I've never seen anything like it before. Whatever do you think those men keep it there for? Seems funny, doesn't it, in a place like this?'

Tom sat up with a jerk. 'Some sort of *machinery*!' he said in amazement. 'What, in that old hut on that desolate mountainside, where there are only a few sheep? How would they get machinery there? There's no road.'

'There's a rough road the other side of the mountain,' said Sandy. 'Easy enough to go over the top, and get down to the path that way – and there's a good motor-road a bit further down the other side, too.'

Tom whistled. His eyes grew bright. 'I wonder if we've hit on something peculiar!' he said. 'We'll tell your father, and see what he says. Perhaps those two men are spies!'

'Don't be silly,' said Sandy. 'What would spies do here, among the mountains? There's nothing to spy on! Anyway, my father is away now.'

'All right, Mr Know-all,' said Tom. 'But we might as well tell your father when he comes back, all the same!'

CHAPTER 3

A Chapter of Quarrels

The next day the children began lessons with Miss Mitchell. Tom was most disgusted.

'Have I got to learn from a woman?' he said. 'I've been used to going to a boys' school. I don't want to learn from a woman.'

'Well, Sandy does,' said Mrs MacLaren with a laugh. 'And he's a pretty hefty boy, isn't he? There is no school here, you see, and until the war is over Sandy must stay at home.'

So Tom and Sheila joined Sandy and Jeanie in the schoolroom with Miss Mitchell – and they soon found a way of paying back the two Scottish children for the long walk of the day before! Tom was far ahead of Sandy in arithmetic, and Sheila's writing was beautiful – quite different from Jeanie's scrawl.

'Good gracious! Is that as far as you've got in arithmetic!' said Tom, looking at Sandy's book. 'I did those sums *years* ago! You *are* a baby!'

Sandy scowled down at his book. He knew he was not good at arithmetic. Miss Mitchell had struggled with him for years.

'Go to your place, Tom,' said Miss Mitchell briskly. 'Everybody isn't the same. Some are good at one thing and some are good at another. We'll see if your geography is as good as your arithmetic! Perhaps it isn't!'

But it was! Tom was a clever boy, and Sheila was a sharp little girl, who read easily and beautifully, and who wrote as well as Miss Mitchell herself.

'I can see that Sheila and I are going to be the top of the class!' said Tom slyly to Sandy, as they went out at eleven o'clock for a break in their lessons. 'You may be able to beat us at climbing mountains, Sandy – but we'll beat you at lesson-time! Why, Jeanie writes like a baby!'

'I *don't*!' said Jeanie, almost in tears.

'Yes, you do,' said Sheila. 'Why, at home even the *first* class could write better than you can! And you don't even know your twelve times table yet!'

This was quite true. Jeanie did not like lessons, and she had never troubled to try really hard to learn all her tables. Poor Miss Mitchell had been in despair over her many times.

But Jeanie was not going to have her English

cousins laughing at her. She made up her mind to learn all her tables perfectly as soon as she could. This was hard for her, because Jeanie would not usually spend any of her playtime doing anything but climbing the hills, swimming in the river, and driving round the lanes in the pony-trap or the waggonette.

Secretly Miss Mitchell was pleased that Tom and Sheila were ahead of Jeanie and Sandy. Now perhaps her two pupils would feel ashamed, and would work much harder.

'And it won't do Tom and Sheila any harm to find that they can't do the walking and climbing that our two can,' thought Miss Mitchell. 'After a few quarrels they will all settle down and be happy together.'

The two dogs eyed one another and tried to boast to one another in their own way. Paddy could do plenty of tricks, and whenever he wanted a biscuit he sat up on his hind legs in a comical way. Then Tom would put a biscuit on his nose, and say, 'Trust, Paddy, trust!'

Paddy would not eat the biscuit until Tom said 'Paid for!' Then he would toss the biscuit into the air, catch it, and gobble it up.

Mack watched this trick scornfully. *He* wasn't going to do any tricks for *his* food! Not he! If he wanted anything extra he'd go out and catch a rabbit. He was very proud of the fact that he could run as fast as a rabbit, and had three times brought a rabbit home to Sandy. Could Paddy do that? Mack barked to Paddy and asked him.

Paddy didn't answer. He lay curled up by Tom's feet, his eyes on Mack, ready to fly at him if he came any nearer. Mack whined scornfully, and then got up. He meant to show Paddy what he could do.

'Woof?' he said. Paddy got up too. He knew that Mack wanted him to go out with him, and though he was still on his guard, he thought it would be fun to go into the hills with this dog, who knew the way about.

'Look at that!' said Sandy in surprise. That's the first time that Paddy has gone with Mack without flying at him.'

The two dogs trotted out of doors, Paddy a good way behind. He could see the tiniest wag in Mack's tail and so he trusted him – but if that wag stopped, then Paddy was ready to pounce on him!

Out of the corner of his eye Mack saw Paddy's tail too. He could see the tiniest wag there also. Good. As long as that little wag was there, Mack knew that Paddy would not fling himself on him!

So, each watching the other carefully, the dogs went out on the hills. And then Mack began to show off to Paddy. He spied a rabbit under a bush and gave chase. The rabbit tore down a burrow. Mack started up another one and that went down a burrow too. Then Paddy started up a young rabbit, but it was away and up the hill before he had even seen which way it went!

'Woof! Watch me!' barked Mack, and he tore after a big rabbit so fast that he snapped at its white bobtail before it could get down a burrow. Mack walked back to Paddy, with the bit of white fluff still in his mouth.

Paddy turned his head away, pretending not to look, and then began to scratch himself. *He* wasn't going to tell this boastful dog that he thought it was jolly clever to catch a rabbit's tail — though secretly he couldn't help admiring Mack very much for his speed and strength. After he had scratched himself well, he got up and trotted back to the house.

'I'm tired of this silly game,' his tail seemed to say to Mack. Mack followed him in, disappointed. Paddy waited till both dogs were in the room, and then he stood on his hind legs and shut the door! This was another of his tricks, and people always thought it was very clever.

'Goodness! Did you see Paddy shut the door?' said Jeanie, quite astonished. 'Mack! *You* can't do that, old boy! You'd better learn!'

Mack was angry. He growled. What! Here he had just been smart enough to catch a rabbit's tail — and now this silly dog had shut the door and been praised for a stupid thing like *that*. Dear me – and Sheila was giving him a biscuit for his cleverness! Well, why didn't Sandy give *him* a biscuit for his smartness with rabbits?

And so both the dogs and the children were angry with the other's boasting, and would not be friends. Out-of-doors the Scottish cousins were far and away better than the English pair, and could run faster, jump higher and climb further – but indoors Tom and Sheila shone. Their lessons were done more quickly and better than their cousins', and they could learn anything by heart in a few minutes.

'It takes me half an hour to learn this bit of poetry,' grumbled Sandy. He was bent over 'Horatius keeps the Bridge'. He liked the story in it, but it was so difficult to learn.

'How slow you are!' laughed Tom. 'It took me just five minutes. I can say it straight off now – listen!'

'Oh be quiet, you boaster!' growled Sandy, putting his hands over his ears. 'I wish you'd never come! You make Miss Mitchell think that Jeanie and I are as stupid as sheep, and she's always scolding us.'

There was silence. Tom and Sheila said nothing at all. Sandy began to feel uncomfortable. He looked up. Tom had gone very red, and Sheila looked as if she was going to cry.

Tom got up and spoke stiffly. 'I'm sorry you wish we'd never come. We didn't think we were as bad as all that. But seeing that you have said what you really thought, I'll also say what *I* think. I wish we had never come too. Sheila and I have done our best to keep up with you in your walking and climbing because we didn't want you to think we were weak and feeble. But we are not used to mountains and it would have been kinder of you if you'd let us go a bit slower at first. However, I suppose that's too much to expect.'

'And *I'd* like to say something too!' burst out Sheila. 'You're always boasting about your wonderful mountains and the brown bur-r-rns, and the purple heather-r-r-r – but we would rather have the things we know. We'd like to see the big London buses we love, and our tall policemen, and to see the trains. We'd like to see more people about, and to go in the parks and play with our own friends at the games we know. It's p-p-p-perfectly horrid b-b-being here – and I w-w-w-want my m-m-m-mother!'

She burst into tears. Jeanie was horrified. Had they really been as unkind as all that? She ran over to Sheila and tried to put her arms round her cousin. But Sheila pushed her away fiercely. Tom went over and hugged his sister.

'Cheer up,' he said. 'When the war's over we'll go back home. Sandy and Jeanie will be glad to

be rid of us then – but we'll make the best of it till we go.'

Sandy wanted to say a lot of things but he couldn't say a word. He was ashamed of himself. After all, his cousins were his guests. How *could* he have said to them that he wished they had never come? What would his mother and father say if they knew? Scottish people were famous for the welcome they gave to friends.

Tom thought that Sandy was sulking, and he looked at him in disgust. 'I'm sorry Sheila and I are a bit more forward in our lessons than you,' he said. 'But we can't help that any more than you can help knowing your old mountains better than we do. Sheila, do stop crying. Here comes Aunt Jessie.'

Jeanie looked up in alarm. If Mother came in and wanted to know why Sheila was crying and found out – my goodness, there would be trouble! She and Sandy would be sent to bed at once, and have nothing but bread and water!

Sheila stopped crying at once. She bent her head over her book. Tom went to his place and began to mutter his poetry to himself – so when Mother came into the room she saw four children all working hard, and did not know that two of them were ashamed and frightened, that one was angry and hurt and the fourth one was very miserable and homesick.

She looked round. 'What, still doing lessons!' she said.

'It's some poetry Miss Mitchell gave us to learn before we went out,' explained Tom. 'We've nearly finished.'

'Well, finish it this evening,' said Mother. 'It's half-past two now, and a lovely day. Would you all like to take your tea out somewhere on the hills, and have a picnic? You won't be able to do it much longer, when the mists come down.'

'Oh yes, Mother, do let's have a picnic!' cried Jeanie, flinging down her book. She always loved a picnic. 'We'll go and find some blackberries.'

'Very well,' said Mother. 'Go and get ready and I'll pack up your tea.'

She went out. Jeanie spoke to Sheila. 'It was nice of you not to let Mother see you were crying,' she said. Sheila said nothing. She looked miserably at Jeanie. She did not want to climb mountains for a picnic. But there was no help for it. It was such a hilly country that sooner or later you had to climb, no matter in what direction you went!

The girls went to their room. Jeanie pulled out some comfortable old shoes and took them to Sheila. 'Look,' she said. 'Wear these, Sheila. They are old and strong, much better for climbing than the shoes you wear. Mother is getting some strong shoes for you next time she goes into the town.'

They fitted Sheila well. Jeanie gave her an old tammy instead of a straw hat. Then they went downstairs to find the boys.

Sandy still hadn't said a word to Tom. He just couldn't. He always found it very difficult to say he was sorry about anything. But he found a good stick and handed it to Tom, knowing that it would make climbing a good deal easier.

Tom took it – but he put it in a corner of the room when Sandy was not looking! He would dearly have loved to take it, but he wasn't going to have Sandy thinking he needed a stick, like an old man! Jeanie saw him put the stick away and she went to Sandy.

'Sandy!' she whispered. 'Tom would like the stick, I know, and so would Sheila – but they won't have them if they think we don't take them too. So let's take one each, and then the others won't mind.'

This was rather clever of Jeanie! For as soon as Tom saw that Jeanie and Sandy had also found sticks for themselves he at once went to take his from the corner where he had put it! After all, if his cousins used a stick, there was no reason why he shouldn't as well!

They set off. They allowed both dogs to come, for although they were still not good friends the two dogs put up with one another better now.

Tom and Sandy carried a bag each on their backs, full of the picnic things.

'I say! Let's go up to that funny old hut again, and see if those two men are still there!' said Tom, who always liked an adventure. 'I'd like to peep into that back room if I could, and find that machine that Sandy saw.'

'But isn't that too far?' said Jeanie, anxious to show that she could consider others. Tom shook his head stoutly. He was beginning to get used to the hills now.

'I can help Sheila over the bad bits,' he said, 'and now that she's got strong shoes on, and a good stick, she'll be all right, won't you, Sheila?'

'Yes,' said Sheila bravely – though her heart sank at the thought of the long climb again.

'All right then,' said Sandy. 'We'll go up to the hut and see what we can find!'

CHAPTER 4

A WALK AND A SURPRISE

They set off. Sheila did not find the climb so hard as she thought. She was getting used to walking in the hilly country now, and besides, Jeanie's shoes were well-made for climbing and were very comfortable. So Sheila walked well, and began to enjoy herself.

'We'll have our tea when we get to that clump of birch trees,' said Jeanie, when they had climbed for some time. 'There's a marvellous view from there. We can see the steamers going by, it's such a clear day!'

So, when they reached the birches, they all sat down and undid the picnic bags. There were tomato sandwiches, hard-boiled eggs, with a screw of salt to dip them into, brown bread and butter, buttered scones, and some fine currant cake. The children ate hungrily, and looked far away to where the sea shone blue in the autumn sunshine.

'There goes a steamer!' said Jeanie, pointing to where a grey steamer slid over the water. 'And there's another.'

'Over there is where the *Yelland* went down,' said Sandy, pointing to the east. 'And not far from it the *Harding* was torpedoed too. I hope those steamers will be all right that we are watching now.'

'Of course they will,' said Tom lazily. 'I bet there's no submarine round about here!'

Jeanie cleared up the litter and packed the bits of paper back into the bags. Her mother was always very strict about litter, and it had to be brought back and burnt, never left lying about.

'Well, what about creeping up to see if we can spot what's in that back room?' said Tom, getting up. 'I'm well rested now. What about you, Sheila?'

'Sheila can stay here with me,' said Jeanie, quickly. 'I don't want to go any further today. We'll wait here till you come back.'

Sheila looked at Jeanie gratefully. She was tired, and did not really want to go any further – but she would not have said so for anything!

Sandy looked at Jeanie in amazement, and was just going to tease her for being lazy, when his sister winked quickly at him. That wink said as plainly as anything – 'Sheila's tired but won't say so – so I'll pretend I am, and then she won't mind staying here.'

'All right, Jeanie,' said Sandy. 'Tom and I will go – and we'll take the two dogs.'

So off went the two boys, each with his stick, though Sandy kept forgetting to use his, and tucked it under his arm. Tom was glad to have the help of his, though, and it made a great difference to the climb.

When they had almost come in sight of the old cottage, Tom stopped. 'I think one of us had better stay here a few minutes with the dogs,' he said. 'The other can creep through the heather and find out whether the men are about – and that dog they spoke of. *I* don't want to be a dog's dinner!'

'All right,' said Sandy. 'Take the dogs, Tom. I'll go. I know the way better than you do.'

So Tom held the two dogs, and Sandy wriggled through the heather silently until he came in sight of the old cottage. No one seemed to be about. The door was shut. No dog barked.

Sandy wriggled closer. Not a sound was to be heard. No smoke came from the chimney. Sandy suddenly got up and ran to the old cottage. He peered in at the front window. The place was empty, though the furniture was still there.

It only took the boy a minute or two to make sure that no one, man or dog, was about. He ran to the edge of the heather and whistled to Tom. Up he came with the two dogs.

'There's no one here,' said Sandy. 'We'll go in and I'll show you that funny machinery with all its knobs and handles and things.'

They tried the door. It was locked! Sandy put his hefty shoulder to it and pushed – but the lock was good and strong and would not give an inch.

'They've put a new lock on it,' said the boy in disappointment. 'It never used to have a lock at all. Well, let's go and look in through the back window.'

They went round to the back of the cottage. But there they had a surprise!

'They've boarded up the window inside!' said Sandy in amazement. 'We can't see a thing! Not a thing! Oh blow! I did want to show you what was in that little room, Tom.'

'It's funny,' said Tom thoughtfully, rubbing his chin and frowning. 'Why should they do that? It means that the machinery, whatever it is, is still in there, and they've boarded it up in case we come back and spy around. I do wish we could get into the house.'

But it was no good wishing. The door was locked and bolted, the one front window was fastened tightly, and the back one was boarded up so well that not even a chink was left for peeping.

'Well, we can't see anything, that's certain,' said Tom. 'Let's go and have a look at that stream coming out of the hillside through that rock, Sandy. I'd like to see that again.'

The boys went there. The water still poured out of the curious hole – but there was not so much of it as before.

'That's because we haven't had so much rain this week,' explained Sandy. Tom nodded. He went to the hole and peered into it. 'If the water goes down much more we could easily get in there,' he said. 'I'd love to see where that water comes from. I read a book written by a Frenchman, Sandy, who explored heaps of underground streams and caves in France, and crawled through holes like that.'

'What did he find?' asked Sandy, interested.

'He found wonderful caves and underground halls and pits, and he found where some mysterious rivers had their beginnings,' said Tom. 'I'll show you the book when we get home. You know, if only we could get past that spring pouring out from the rock, we might find extraordinary caverns where no foot had ever trodden before!'

Tom was getting excited. His eyes shone, and he made Sandy feel thrilled too. 'Might there be a cave or something in this mountain then?' he asked.

'There might be heaps,' said Tom. 'And maybe somewhere in this great mountain is the beginning of the River Spelter. You told me that it comes out from underground and that no one knows where it rises.'

Sandy's eyes shone now. This was the most exciting thing he had ever heard of. 'Tom, we *must* explore this,' he said. 'We must! If only those men weren't here – they will send us away if they see us. I wish I knew what they were up to.'

'So do I,' said Tom. 'When your father comes back, we'll tell him about them, Sandy, and about the odd machinery they've hidden in that back room.'

A rabbit suddenly appeared on the hillside and looked cheekily at the two dogs, who were sitting quietly by the boys. At once both Paddy and Mack barked loudly and tore at the rabbit.

It did a strange thing. It shot up the hillside, leapt over the boys, and then disappeared into a burrow just beside the spring that gushed from the rock. And then Paddy did an even stranger thing!

He shot after the rabbit – but was stopped by the water. He leapt right over the water, saw the hole in the rock through which the spring flowed – and shot into the hole! He thought the rabbit had gone there!

He didn't come out. He disappeared completely. The two boys gaped at one another, and then Tom called his dog sharply.

'Paddy! Paddy! Come here!'

No Paddy came. Only a frightened whining could be heard from inside the hole. Paddy must have got right through the water and be sitting somewhere beyond.

'Paddy! Come out!' cried Tom anxiously. 'You got in – so you can get out! Come on now!'

But Paddy was terrified. The noise of the water inside the rock was tremendous, and the dog was terribly afraid. He had managed to scramble to a rocky shelf above the flow of the spring, and was sitting there, trembling. He could hardly hear the shouts of his master, because of the noise the water made.

'*Now* what are we to do?' said Tom, in dismay. 'He's right inside that rock. Paddy! PADDY, you idiot!'

But Paddy did not appear. Sandy looked worried. They must get the dog somehow.

Tom looked at Sandy. 'Well, I suppose he will come out sometime,' he said. 'Had we better wait any longer? The girls will be getting worried.'

'We can't leave your dog,' said Sandy. He knew that Tom loved Paddy as much as he loved Mack. Mack was looking astonished. He could not imagine where Paddy had gone!

Sandy climbed up to the rock, and looked into the hole. The rushing water wetted him, and spray flew into his face.

'I believe I could wriggle through the water today,' he said. 'It's not very deep and not very strong. I could find old Paddy and push him out for you.'

'Oh no, Sandy,' said Tom. 'You'd get soaked, and you might hurt yourself. You don't know what's behind that spring!'

Sandy was stripping off his clothes. He grinned at Tom. 'I don't mind if I *do* get soaked now,' he said. 'I'll just hang myself out to dry, if I do!'

CHAPTER 5

A RESCUE AND A
STRANGE DISCOVERY

Sandy climbed right up to the hole again, and then began to push himself into it. It was more than big enough for his body. As he wriggled, the cold water soaked him, and sometimes his face was under the surface, so that he had to hold his breath. His body blocked up the light that came in from the hole, and everything looked black as night. It was very strange.

He felt about as he went through the hole. It widened almost at once, behind the opening, and became higher and more spacious. The water became shallower too. Sandy sat up in the water, and felt about with his hand. He felt the rocky ceiling a little above him, and on one side was a rocky shelf. His hand touched wet hair!

'Paddy!' he cried. 'You poor thing! Go on out of the hole, you silly!'

His voice was almost drowned in the sound of the rushing water around him, but Paddy heard it and was comforted. He jumped down into the water beside Sandy. Sandy pushed him towards the hole.

Paddy was taken by the swirl of the water and lost his balance. The water took him like a floating log and he was rushed to the opening, struggling with all his feet. He shot out with the spring, and fell at Tom's feet.

Tom was delighted. He picked up the wet dog and hugged him, and then Paddy struggled down to shake the water from his hair. Mack came up and sniffed him in astonishment.

'Been swimming?' he seemed to say. 'What an extraordinary idea!'

Sandy was still in the rocky hole. He was getting used to the darkness now. He sat up on the shelf where he had found Paddy, and felt about with his hands. Then he made his way a little further up the stream. The rocky ceiling got quickly higher – and then Sandy found himself in a great cave, at the bottom of which the stream rushed along with a noise that echoed all around. It was so dark that Sandy could hardly see the shape of the cave. He only sensed that it rose high and was wide and spacious. He was filled with astonishment and excitement, and went back to tell Tom.

But meanwhile something was happening outside! Tom had heard voices, and, peeping

round the bend, he had seen in the distance the two men returning to their cottage! With them was a large dog.

Tom called in through the hole. 'Sandy! Sandy! Quick! Come back!'

Sandy was already coming back. He sat down in the water when the ceiling fell low, and then, as it became lower still, the boy had to lie full length in the water, and wriggle along like that, the stream sometimes going right over his face. He got to the opening at last, and Tom helped him down.

'Sandy! Hurry! The men are back!' whispered Tom. 'They've got a dog too, and he may hear us at any moment. Put on your things quickly.'

Sandy tried to be quick. But his body was cold from the icy water, and he could not make his hands pull on his things quickly over his wet body. He shook and shivered with the cold, and Tom did his best to help him to dress.

He was just getting on his coat when the men's dog came sniffing round the corner! When he saw the boys and the dogs he stood still, and the fur on his neck rose high with rage! He barked loudly.

'Quick!' said Tom to Sandy. 'We must go. Let's go down this way and maybe the men won't see us!'

So the two boys hurried round a bend, where

bracken grew tall, and began to make their way through it. The dog still barked loudly, and the two men came running to him.

'What is it? Who is it?' cried one of them. 'Go on, find him, find him!'

The fat man shouted something too, but the boys could not understand what he said. They were creeping down the hillside, glad that the men had not yet seen them. But the dog heard them, and came bounding after them.

'Now we're done for!' groaned Tom, as he saw the big dog leaping down towards them. He grasped his stick firmly. But someone else stood before him! It was Paddy, his wet fur bristling, and his throat almost bursting with fierce growls. Mack joined him, his teeth bared. Side by side the two dogs glared at the enemy, who, when he saw two of them, stopped still and considered. He was bigger than either – but they were two!

The men were following their dog. 'Come on, Tom,' whispered Sandy. 'Let the dogs settle it for us. We must get back to the girls quickly.'

They wriggled through the bracken and heather, slid down a stony piece unseen, and then made their way to where the girls were waiting anxiously. The boys had been a very long time.

'Sh!' said Sandy, as Jeanie opened her mouth to shout a welcome. And just as he said that a tremendous noise broke out – a noise of barking and howling and whining and yelping and growling and snarling!

'Good gracious!' said Jeanie, starting up. 'Are the dogs fighting?'

'Yes – fighting a big dog together!' said Sandy. 'Come on, we must go whilst the dogs are keeping off the men. They haven't seen us yet and we don't want them to.'

'But will the dogs be all right?' panted Sheila as they ran down the hillside.

'Of course!' said Sandy. 'Our Mack is more than a match for two other dogs, and I reckon your Paddy is too!'

The children stopped when they reached a big gorse bush, and sat down behind it, panting. They were safe there, for an old shepherd's shelter was nearby, and Loorie, the shepherd, was pottering about in the distance. In a few hurried words the boys told the girls all that had happened.

Tom stared when Sandy told of the cave behind the rock where the spring gushed out. 'I was right then!' he cried. 'I say, what fun! We must go and explore that when we get a chance. If only those men weren't there.'

'Perhaps they won't be there long, once my father hears about them,' said Sandy grimly. 'I think they are spies of some sort. I guess the police would like to see what is in their back room too!'

'I wish those dogs would come back,' said Sheila, looking worried, for she hated to think that Paddy might be bitten by the big dog.

No sooner had she spoken than the two dogs appeared, looking extremely pleased with themselves! Paddy's right ear was bleeding, and Mack's left ear looked the worse for wear – but otherwise they seemed quite all right.

They trotted up to the children together, and sat down, looking proud and pleased. Mack licked Paddy's ear. Paddy sniffed in a friendly way at Mack and then, putting out a paw, pawed him as if he wanted a game.

'Why, they're good friends now!' cried Jeanie in surprise. 'They like each other!'

Tom and Sandy looked at one another. Jeanie looked at Sheila.

'It's time *we* were friends too,' said Tom, with a red face. 'Thanks, Sandy, for rescuing Paddy from that hole. It was jolly good of you – getting into that icy-cold water and wriggling up a narrow rocky hole. You're a good sort.'

'So are you,' said Sandy. 'I'm sorry for what I said. I didn't mean it. I was only mad because you were better at arithmetic than I was. I'm glad you came, really.'

'Shake!' said Tom, with a laugh, and he held

out his hand to Sandy. 'We're friends now, and we'll stick by each other, won't we – just like the two dogs!'

The girls stared at the boys, glad to see that they were friends now. Jeanie held out her hand to Sheila. She would have liked to hug her, but she thought it looked grander to shake hands like the boys. Sheila solemnly shook her hand, and then they all began to laugh.

CHAPTER 6

A DISAPPOINTMENT – AND A PICNIC

Things began to happen very quickly after that exciting day. For one thing Captain MacLaren, Sandy's father, returned home on forty-eight hours' leave, and the children and Mrs MacLaren told him about the mysterious men in the old cottage on the mountain.

Captain MacLaren was astonished and puzzled. He was inclined to think that Sandy was making too much of the curious 'machinery' he had seen in the back room. However, when he heard that one man had called the other 'Carl,' he decided that he had better tell the police.

'Carl is a German name,' he said. 'I can't imagine why German spies could possibly want to hide themselves away on such a lonely hillside, but you never know! They may be up to something odd. I'll ring up the police.'

He did so – and two solemn Scots policemen

came riding out to Kidillin House on their bicycles, with large notebooks and stumpy pencils to take down all the children said.

'We'll go up to the cottage and investigate, captain,' said the sergeant, shutting his notebook with a snap. 'It's a wee bit unlikely we'll be finding anything to make a noise about, but we'll go.'

They knew where the cottage was, and they set off to find it that afternoon. The children were very much excited. Miss Mitchell could hardly get them to do any sums, French, or history at all. Even her star pupil, Tom, made all kinds of silly mistakes, and when he said that there were 240 shillings in a pound, instead of 240 pence, the governess put down her pencil in despair.

'This won't do,' she said. 'You are not thinking of what you are doing. What *are* you thinking of?'

But the four children wouldn't tell her! They were thinking of the exciting cave that Sandy had discovered behind the stream! They hadn't said a word about this to the grown-ups, because they were afraid that if they did they might be forbidden to explore it – and how could they bear to promise such a thing?

'We'll tell Mother as soon as we know exactly what's behind that hole,' said Sandy. 'We'll take our torches, and we'll explore properly. We might find strange cave pictures done by men hundreds of years ago! We might find old stone arrowheads and all kinds of exciting things!'

Sandy had been reading Tom's book. This book told of the true adventures of a Frenchman in underground caves and rivers, and of all the wonderful pictures he had found drawn on the walls and ceilings of the hidden caves. Sandy was simply longing to do some exploring himself now.

Miss Mitchell decided that it was no use doing any more lessons until the policeman came back from the old cottage. She was feeling a bit excited herself, and guessed what the children's feelings must be like. So she told them to shut their books, and go to do some gardening. Sandy and Jeanie each had their own gardens, and Tom and Sheila had been given a patch too.

'It is time to dig up your old beans and to cut down your summer plants, Sandy,' said Miss Mitchell. 'Tom, you can help the gardener to sweep up the leaves. Sheila, you can help Jeanie to get down the beanpoles.'

The children ran off, shouting in joy. From the garden they would be able to see the police-men when they came down from the mountain.

'They'll have the two spies with them!' said Sandy.

'Yes, and maybe they'll be handcuffed together,' said Tom, sweeping up the leaves as if they were spies! 'I wonder if they'll make the dog a prisoner too!'

'I guess our two dogs gave him a rough time!' said Jeanie. She looked at Mack and Paddy, who were tearing round and round after each other. Jeanie had doctored their ears well, and they were almost healed already. She was very good with animals. 'They're jolly good friends now!' said Jeanie, pleased. 'I'm glad we don't have to tie up first one and then another.'

'I wonder how the police will get that machinery down the mountain,' said Tom, stopping his sweeping for a moment.

'Same way as it was got up, I expect!' said Sandy. 'On somebody's back! I expect it was taken up in pieces from the road the other side of the mountain.'

'Look!' said Sheila suddenly. 'Here come the policemen! Aunt! Uncle! Miss Mitchell! Here come the policemen.'

In great excitement the children ran to the gate. But to their disappointment they saw that the two policemen coming down the hillside were alone. The men were not with them!

'I wonder why,' said Tom.

'Perhaps they weren't there,' suggested Jeanie.

The policemen came up to Kidillin House and

smiled as the children rained questions on them. Only when Captain MacLaren came out to see them did they say what had happened.

'Yes, sir, there are two men there all right,' said the sergeant. 'They say that they left London because of their fear of air-raids, and took that little cottage for safety. I asked them to let me look all over it – and there's no machinery of any sort there. I think yon boy of yours must have imagined it. There's no place round the old cottage where they could hide anything either.'

'I *didn't* imagine it!' cried Sandy. 'I didn't!'

'Did any of the others see it?' asked the sergeant, looking at Tom, Sheila, and Jeanie.

'No,' they said. 'But we saw the windows boarded up!'

'They say they did that for the black-out,' said the second policeman. 'They've curtains for the front room but none for the back.'

'Pooh! As if they'd bother to black-out windows that look right on to the mountain behind!' said Tom, scornfully. 'All a made-up tale!'

'One man is deaf and dumb,' said the sergeant. 'We got all the talk from the dark man.'

That made the children stare even more. Both Tom and Sandy had heard the *two* men talking. Why then did one pretend to be deaf and dumb?

The policemen jumped on to their bicycles and rode off, saluting the captain. The children gathered together in a corner of the garden and began to talk.

'What have they done with the machinery?'

'Why did one pretend to be dumb?'

'What a stupid reason for boarding up the window!'

'I guess I know why one pretended to be dumb! I bet he talks English with a German accent! I bet if he answered the policeman's questions, he would give himself away at once!' This was Tom speaking, and the others listened to him.

'Yes, that's it!' went on the excited boy. 'He's the one called Carl – he's a German all right. It's an old trick to pretend to be dumb if you don't want to give yourself away!'

'And they guessed we might tell the police so they hid their machinery quickly,' said Sandy. 'But didn't have time to unboard the windows.'

'That's it,' said Tom. There was a silence, whilst they all thought quickly.

'Golly! I think I know!' cried Tom, in such an excited voice that they all jumped. 'They've taken it to pieces, and managed somehow to get it into the cave behind the stream! That's what they've done. Somehow or other they must have known about that cave.'

'It would be easy enough to do that, if the two of them worked together,' said Sandy, thinking hard. 'They could wrap the pieces in oiled cloth, tie them to ropes – and then one man could climb back to the cave and pull up the rope whenever the other man tied the packets on to it. It is sure to be able to break down into pieces, that machine – how else could they have got it up to the cottage so secretly?'

'We've hit on their secret all right,' said Tom, and his face glowed. '*Now* what we've got to do is quite simple.'

'What's that?' asked all the others.

'Why, all we've got to do is to go up to the cottage, lie low till the men go shopping or something, and then explore that cave again,' said Tom. 'If we find the machinery is there, we'll know we're right, and we can slip down to the police at once!'

'Oh good!' said Sandy. 'The girls could keep watch for us, Tom, and you and I could take our swim-suits and wriggle through the hole together.'

'Is there time today?' wondered Tom looking at his watch. But there wasn't. It was a nuisance, because all the children were longing to go on with their big adventure – and now they would have to wait till the next day!

Fortunately for them the next day was

Saturday. They begged their governess to let them take their lunch on the hills. Mrs MacLaren had gone to the town to see her husband off once more, and Miss Mitchell was in charge.

'Very well,' said Miss Mitchell. 'I think I'll come with you today. I've nothing much to do.'

The children stared at one another in dismay. If Miss Mitchell came they couldn't do anything! They could not think of a single reason to give her to stop her coming.

'I'll go and ask the cook to get a good lunch ready,' said Miss Mitchell, bustling out to the kitchen. 'I'll pack it up nicely in the picnic bags.'

'Well, isn't that awful!' said Sheila, as the governess went out of the room. 'What *can* we do to stop her coming?'

They thought and thought – but it was no good. She would have to come!

'Well, listen,' said Tom at last. 'After we have had our picnic, you two girls can stay with Miss Mitchell, and Sandy and I will slip off to explore again. That's the only thing we can do.'

'But we wanted to come too!' wailed Sheila.

'Well, you can't!' said Tom. 'Now for goodness' sake don't make a fuss, Sheila, or Miss Mitchell will begin to think something's up!'

But Miss Mitchell didn't guess anything at

all. She packed up the lunch, gave it to the two boys to carry on their backs, and soon they were all ready to start.

'Got your torch, Sandy?' whispered Tom.

'Yes,' whispered back Sandy. 'And I've got my swim-suit on under my clothes too!'

They all set off. They climbed up the sunny hillside, chattering and laughing, picking blackberries as they went. Miss Mitchell was glad to see them all such good friends now, even the two dogs! They chased rabbits, real and imaginery, all the time, and once Paddy got so far down a hole that he had to be pulled out by Tom.

The boys made their way towards the cottage. Miss Mitchell was not sure she wanted to go there.

'Those men won't like us spying around,' she said. 'They probably guess that it is you children who had the police sent up there.'

'Well, we'll not go too near,' said Sandy. 'What about having our lunch here, Miss Mitchell? There's a beautiful view for you to look at.'

Miss Mitchell knew the view well. It was the same one that the children had looked at before, when they watched the steamers going by, far away on the blue sea. They all sat down, glad of a rest.

'There's a steamer,' said Tom.

'Yes,' said Miss Mitchell, looking at it through the pair of field-glasses she had brought. 'I hope it won't be sunk. Those coastal steamers should go in convoys, but they won't be bothered – and two were sunk the other day.'

'What were they?' asked Sandy. 'The *Yelland* and the *Harding*, do you mean?'

'No, two others have been sunk since then,' said Miss Mitchell. 'By a submarine too – so there must be one lurking about somewhere.'

The children looked at the little steamer slipping slowly along, and hoped that it would not be sunk. Miss Mitchell opened the picnic bags and handed out ham sandwiches, tomatoes, hard-boiled eggs, apples, jam-tarts and ginger buns.

'Ooooh! What a gorgeous picnic!' said Sheila, who was rapidly getting as big an appetite as her Scottish cousins. There was creamy milk to drink too. The dogs had one large biscuit each and little bits of ham that the children pulled from their sandwiches. Everybody was very happy.

'Goodness me, the sun's hot!' said Miss Mitchell, after they had all eaten as much as they could. 'You had better have a little rest before we go on – we really can't climb higher, on top of our enormous lunch!'

She lay back on the warm heather and put her hat over her eyes. The children sat as still as mice. The same thought came into everyone's head. Would Miss Mitchell go to sleep?

For five minutes nobody said a single word. Even the dogs lay quiet. Then Jeanie gave a little cough. Miss Mitchell didn't stir. Jeanie spoke in a low voice. 'Miss Mitchell!'

No answer from Miss Mitchell. Jeanie leaned over her governess, and lifted Miss Mitchell's hat up gently so that she could see if the governess was really asleep.

Her eyes were fast shut and she was breathing deeply. Jeanie nodded to the others. Very quietly they got up from the heather, shaking their fingers at the two dogs to warn them to be quiet. They climbed up higher, rounded a bend in the hillside, and then began to giggle.

'Good!' said Tom, at last. 'We've got away nicely. Now come on quickly, everyone. We haven't a minute to lose!'

They climbed quickly towards the old cottage, keeping a good look-out as they went. Would the two men be about? Would they be able to do any exploring? They all felt tremendously excited, and their hearts beat loudly and fast.

CHAPTER 7

MISS MITCHELL IS
VERY CROSS

Slowly and quietly the children crept over the
heather that surrounded the cottage. Mack
and Paddy crept with them, joining in what they
thought was some new game.

No one was about. The dog was not to be seen
either. 'I'll just creep over to the cottage and see
what I can see!' whispered Sandy. So off he went,
running quietly to the hut. He peeped cautiously
in at a window – and then drew back very
quickly indeed.

He came back to the others. 'The two men are
there,' he whispered. 'But they are sound asleep,
like Miss Mitchell! This must be a sleepy afternoon! Come on – we'll go to the underground
burn, and see if we can get into the cave and look
round before the men wake up.'

In great delight the four children crept
quietly off to where the big rock jutted out,

through which the water fell down the mountain-side. But when they came in sight of it, what a shock they got!

Tied up beside the rock was the big dog!

The children stopped in dismay. Tom pushed them back, afraid that the dog would see or hear them. They stared at one another, half-frightened.

'It's no good trying any exploring this after-noon!' said Tom, frowning in disappointment. 'Absolutely no good at all. But it shows one thing plainly – they're afraid we may guess their hiding-place and explore it – so they've put the dog there to guard it!'

'Well, we can't possibly get past that big brute,' said Sandy. 'I wonder now if there are any signs of trampling round about the burn there, Tom. If they've hidden anything in that cave, they'd have to stand around the rock a good bit, and the footmarks would show. I've a good mind to creep nearer and see.'

'No, let *me*,' said Tom at once. He always liked to be the one to do things if he could – and Sandy had done the exploring last time! Tom felt it was his turn.

'Tom! Come back!' whispered Sandy, as Tom crept forward on hands and knees. 'I can go much more quietly than you!'

But Tom would not turn back. It was a pity

he didn't – for suddenly he knelt on a dry twig which cracked in two like a pistol shot!

The dog, lying quietly by the rock, raised up its head at once and then leapt to its feet, sniffing the air. Tom crouched flat – but the dog saw him. It began to bark loudly, and the mountain-side rang and echoed with its loud voice.

'Quick! Get down the slope, back to Miss Mitchell!' said Sandy. 'Those men will be out in a minute!'

Sandy was right. The two men woke up at once when they heard the barking of the dog. The door of the cottage opened and out they ran. One of them shouted loudly. 'What is it, Digger, what it it?'

Then he saw the children disappearing down the hillside and with a cry of rage he followed them. 'Loose the dog!' he yelled to the other man. The children tore away as fast as they could, slipping and sliding as they went.

The dog was loosed – but as soon as he was faced once more by the two dogs who had beaten him the other day he dropped his tail and refused to go after the children. The man beat him, but it was no use. Digger was afraid of Mack and Paddy.

But the first man was not afraid of anything! He plunged down the hillside after the children, and just as they reached the place where they had left Miss Mitchell, he caught them up.

Miss Mitchell awoke in a hurry when she heard such a noise of scrambling and shouting. She sat up and looked round. The children ran up to her – and the man came up in a rage.

'What are these children doing here?' he shouted. 'I tell you, I'll whip them all if they come spying round here. Can't a man be left in peace?'

'I don't know what you are talking about,' said Miss Mitchell firmly. 'We came up on the hills for a picnic, and we have as much right here as you have. Please go away at once, or I will report you to the police.'

The man glared at Miss Mitchell. He began to shout again, but when Miss Mitchell repeated that she would certainly tell the police of his threats to her children, he muttered something and went back up the hillside.

Miss Mitchell was very angry with them. 'So you slipped off up to the cottage when I was having a little nap, did you?' she scolded. 'Now you see what has happened! You have made enough trouble for those two men already by telling made-up tales about them – and now you go prowling round their cottage again! You will promise me not to go there again.'

The children looked at one another in dismay. Just what they hoped wouldn't happen!

'Very well,' said Sandy sulkily. 'I promise not to go to the cottage again.'

'So do I,' said Tom. The girls promised too. Miss Mitchell gathered up the picnic things, and said that they must all return home. She really was very cross.

'Miss Mitchell, those weren't made-up tales,' said Sandy, as they went down the mountainside. 'You shouldn't say that. You know we speak the truth.'

'I don't want to hear any more about it,' said the governess. 'It is most unpleasant to have a man roaring and shouting at us like that, because of your stupid behaviour. You know quite well that I would not have allowed you to go to the cottage if you had asked me.'

Miss Mitchell was cross all that day. But the next day was better, and the children went to church glad that Miss Mitchell seemed to have forgotten about the day before. She had not told their mother about them, so that was good.

When they came out of church there was half an hour before lunch. In the distance the children saw Loorie, the old shepherd. Sandy was fond of him, and asked Miss Mitchell if they might go and talk to him.

Loorie was doctoring a sheep that had a bad leg. He nodded to the children, and smiled at Tom and Sheila when Sandy explained that they were his cousins.

'This is an easy time of year for you, isn't it, Loorie?' asked Sandy.

'Oh aye,' said the old man, rubbing the sheep's leg with some horrid-smelling black ointment. 'The winter's the busy time, when the lambing's on.'

He went on to tell Tom and Sheila of all the happenings of the year. The two town children listened in great interest. They could hardly understand the Scottish words the old man used, but they loved to hear them.

'Did you lose any lambs this year, Loorie?' asked Sandy.

'Aye, laddie, I lost too many,' said Loorie. 'And do you ken where I lost them? Down the old pot-hole on the mountain up there!'

'What old pot-hole?' asked Tom, puzzled.

'Oh, it's a peculiar place,' explained Sandy. 'There's a big hole up there, that goes down for ever so far. The sheep sometimes fall into it and they can never be got out.'

'It's funny to sit by the hole,' said Jeanie. 'You can hear a rushing sound always coming up it.'

'Folks do say that's the River Spelter,' said Loorie, setting the sheep on its legs again. 'Aye, folks say a mighty lot of things.'

'The Spelter!' said Tom, surprised. 'Why, do you mean that the Spelter goes under the pot-hole you're talking about?'

'Maybe it does and maybe it doesn't,' said the old shepherd, closing his tin of ointment. 'There's funny things in the mountains. Don't you go taking the lassies near that pot-hole, now, Master Sandy!'

'There's Miss Mitchell calling,' said Sandy hurriedly, for he saw by Tom's face that his cousin was longing to go to visit the pot-hole! 'Goodbye, Loorie. We'll see you again soon.'

As they ran back to Miss Mitchell, Tom panted out some questions. 'Where's the pot-hole? Is it anywhere near the underground stream? Do you suppose that's the Spelter that runs beneath the pot-hole, or our stream?'

Sandy didn't know at all. But he knew quite well that before that day was out, Tom would want to go and explore the pot-hole! Sandy wanted to as well.

'I can't think why I didn't remember the pot-hole before,' thought the boy. 'I suppose it was because I've known about it all my life and never thought anything about it.'

CHAPTER 8

DOWN THE POT-HOLE

That afternoon the four children and the dogs set off to the pot-hole. They had talked about it excitedly, and Tom felt sure that if there was water at the bottom, it might be the very same stream that poured out of the hole in the rock. If it was, they could get down the hole and follow it up – and maybe come to the cave from behind.

'And then we can see if the spies have hidden their things there!' cried Sandy. 'We didn't think there could be another way in – but there may be! What a good thing we had that talk to old Loorie this morning.'

They took a good many things with them that afternoon. Both boys had strong ropes tied round their waists. All of them had torches, and Tom had matches and a candle too.

'You see,' he explained, 'if the air is bad, we

can tell it by lighting a candle. If the candle flickers a lot and goes out, we shall know the air is too bad for us. Then we shall have to go back.'

They also had towels with them, because Tom thought they might have to undress and wade through water. They could leave their towels by the pot-hole and dry themselves when they came back. They all felt excited and important. They were out to catch spies, and to find out their secrets!

Sandy took them round the mountain, in the opposite direction to the one they usually went, and at last brought them to the pot-hole.

It certainly was a very odd place. It looked like a wide pit, overgrown with heather and brambles – but Sandy explained that when they climbed down into this pit-like dell, they would come to the real pot-hole, a much narrower pit at one side of the dell.

They climbed down into the dell, and Sandy took them to one side. He kicked away some branches, and there below them was the pot-hole!

'Loorie must have put those branches across to stop the sheep from falling in,' said Sandy. 'Now just sit beside this hole and listen.'

The four of them sat beside the strange hole. It was not very big, not more than a yard wide, and curious bits of blue slate stuck out all around it. The children peered down into the hole, but it was like looking down into an endless well. They could see nothing but blackness.

But they could hear a most mysterious noise coming up to them! It was like the sound of the wind in the trees, but louder and stranger.

'Yes – that's water rushing along all right,' said Tom, sitting up again, his face red with excitement. 'But it sounds to me a bigger noise than our little stream could make. It sounds more like the River Spelter rushing along in the heart of the mountain, down to where it flows out at the foot, in the village of Kidillin!'

'Could we possibly get down there?' asked Sandy doubtfully. 'Would our ropes be long enough? We don't want any accidents! I don't know how we'd be rescued!'

Tom flashed his torch down the hole. 'Look!' he said. 'Do you see down there, Sandy – about seven feet down? There's a sort of rocky shelf. Well, we may find that all the way down there are these rocky bits to help us. If we have a rope firmly round our waists so that we can't fall, we'll be all right. I'll go down first.'

'No, you won't,' said Sandy. 'I'm better used to climbing. Don't forget that it was you who cracked that twig yesterday and gave warning to the dog. If it had been I who was creeping along, the dog would never have known.'

Tom looked angry. Then the frown went from his face and he nodded. 'All right,' he said. 'Perhaps it would be best if you went. You're good at this sort of thing and I've never done it before.'

'The girls are not to come,' said Sandy. 'Not today, at any rate. It looks more dangerous than I thought, and anyway, we'll want someone to look after the ropes for us. We will tie the ends to a tree, and the girls can watch that they don't slip.'

Neither of the girls made any objection to being left at the top. Both of them thought the pot-hole looked horrid! They were quite content to let the boys try it first!

They all felt really excited. Sandy tied the ends of their two strong ropes to the trunk of a stout pine tree. He and Tom knotted the other ends round their waists as firmly as they could. Now, even if they fell, their ropes would hold them, and the girls could pull them up in safety!

Sandy went down the pot-hole first. He let himself slip down to the rocky ledge some way down. His feet caught on it with a jerk. His hands felt about for something to hold.

'Are you all right, Sandy?' asked Tom, flashing his torch down the hole.

'Yes,' said Sandy. 'I'm feeling to see if there's somewhere to put my feet further down.' Sandy was as good as a cat at climbing. He soon found a small ledge for his right foot, and then another for his left.

Bits of slate, stone and soil broke away as he slowly climbed downwards, and fell far below him. The pot-hole did not go straight down, but curved a little now and again, so that it was not so difficult as Sandy had expected to climb down.

'Come on, Tom!' he called. 'If you're careful where to put your feet, it's not too difficult.'

Tom began his climb down too. He found it far more difficult than Sandy, for he was not so used to climbing. His feet slithered and slipped, and he cut his hands when he clutched at stones and earth.

The girls at the top were holding on to the boys' ropes, letting them out gradually. Tom's rope jerked and pulled, but Sandy's rope went down smoothly.

As Sandy went down further and further, the noise of rushing water became louder and louder until he could not even hear his own voice when he called to Tom. Tom was kicking out so many stones and bits of earth that they fell round poor Sandy like a hailstorm!'

'Stop kicking at the sides of the hole!' yelled Sandy. But Tom couldn't help it. Sandy wished he had put on a hat, to stop the pebbles from hitting his head – but soon, at a bend in the hole, he became free of the 'hailstorm,' and went downwards comfortably.

It was the first part that was so steep and difficult. It was easier further down, for rocky ledges stuck out everywhere, making it almost like climbing down a ladder.

The noise of the water was deafening. Sandy thought it was so near that he might step into it at any moment. So he switched on his torch and looked downwards. The black water gleamed up at him, topped with white spray where it flowed over out-jutting rocks. It was further down than he had thought.

As he climbed down to the water, the hole widened tremendously, and became a cave. Sandy jumped down beside the shouting river, and stood there, half-frightened, half-delighted.

It was a strange sight, that underground river! It flowed along between rocky walls, black, strong and noisy. It entered the cave by a low tunnel, which was filled to the roof with the water. The river flowed in a rocky bed and entered another black tunnel just near Sandy – but it did not fill this tunnel to the roof. Sandy flashed his torch into the tunnel, and saw that for some way, at any rate, the roof was fairly high, about up to his head.

There was a rattle of stones about him, and

Tom came sliding down the walls of the pot-hole at a great speed! He had missed his footing and fallen! But he had not far to fall, and fortunately for him, his rope was only just long enough to take him beside Sandy, and it pulled him up with a jerk, before he fell into the water.

'Good gracious!' said Sandy. 'You *are* in a hurry!'

'Phew!' said Tom, loosening the rope a little round his waist. 'That wasn't very pleasant. I'm glad I was fairly near the bottom. My word, the rope did give my waist an awful pull! I say, Sandy! What a marvellous sight this is!'

'The underground world!' said Sandy, flashing his torch around. 'Look at that black rushing river, Tom! We've got to wade down that, through that tunnel – see?'

'Oooh!' said Tom. 'Where do you suppose it goes to?'

'That's what we've got to find out,' said Sandy. 'I think myself that away up that other tunnel there, is the source of the Spelter. It probably begins in a collection of springs all running to the same rocky bed in the mountain, and then rushing down together as a river. But really it's not more than a fast stream here, though it makes enough noise for a river!'

'That's because it is underground, and the echoes are peculiar,' said Tom. 'Also, it is going downhill at a good rate, not flowing gently in an even bed. How deep do you suppose it is, Sandy?'

'We'll have to find out!' said Sandy, beginning to undress. 'Hurry up! Got your torch with you? Well, bring it, and bring the oil-skin bag too, in case we have to swim, and need something waterproof to put our torches in. I've got the candles and matches.'

CHAPTER 9

In the Heart of the Mountain

Both boys stood in their swim-suits. They shivered, for the air was cold. Sandy put one leg into the rushing stream. The water was icy!

'Oooh!' said Sandy, drawing back his leg quickly! 'It's mighty cold, Tom. Just hang on to me a minute, will you, so that I can feel how deep the water is.'

Tom held on to his arms. Sandy slipped a foot into the water again. He went in over his knee, and right up to his waist! Then he felt a solid rocky bottom, and stood up, grinning.

'It's all right!' he said. 'Only up to my waist, Tom. Come on in and we'll explore the tunnel.'

Tom got into the water, and then the two boys began to wade along the noisy stream. It went gradually downwards, and once there was quite a steep drop, making a small waterfall. The boys had to help one another down. It was very cold, for the water was really icy. They were both shivering, and yet felt hot with excitement.

The roof of the tunnel kept about head or shoulder-high. Once the tunnel widened out again into a small cave, and the boys climbed out of the water and did some violent exercises to warm themselves.

They got back into the water again. It suddenly got narrow and deeper. Deeper and deeper it got until the two boys had to swim. And then, oh dear the tunnel roof dipped down and almost reached the surface of the water!

'*Now* what are we to do?' said Tom, in dismay.

'Put your torch into its oil-skin bag, to begin with,' said Sandy, putting his into the bag, next to the candle and box of matches. 'Then it won't get wet. If you'll just wait here for me, Tom, I'll swim underwater a little way and see if the roof rises further on.'

'Well, for goodness' sake be careful,' said Tom, in alarm. 'I hope you've got enough breath to swim under the water *and* back, if the roof doesn't rise! The water may flow for a long way touching the roof.'

'If it does, we can go no further,' said Sandy. 'Don't worry about *me*! I can swim under water for at least a minute!'

He took a deep breath, plunged under the

water, and swam hard. He bobbed his head up, but found that the rocky ceiling still touched the stream. He went on a little way, and then, when he was nearly bursting for breath, he found that the roof lifted, and he could stand with his head out of the water.

He took another deep breath and went back for Tom. 'It's all right,' he gasped, coming up beside him. 'You need to take a jolly good breath though. Take one now and come along quickly.'

Tom began to splutter under the water before he could stick his head up into the air once more and breathe. Sandy couldn't help laughing at him, and Tom was very indignant.

'Just stop laughing!' he said to Sandy. 'I was nearly drowned!'

'Oh no you weren't,' giggled Sandy. 'I could easily have pulled you through, Tom. Come on – the next bit is easy. We can swim or wade. Let's swim and get warm.'

So they swam along in the deep black water for some way – and then the tunnel widened out into a great underground hall. It was an odd place. Strange stones gleamed in the light of their torches. Phosphorescent streaks shone in the rocky walls, and here and there curious things hung down from the ceiling rather like icicles.

'Ooh, isn't it odd?' whispered Tom – and at

once his whisper came back to him in strange echoes. 'Isn't it odd, isn't it odd – odd – odd?' The whole place seemed to be full of his whispering.

'It's magnificent!' said Sandy, revelling in the strangeness of it. 'See how those stones gleam? I wonder if they're valuable. And look at the shining streaks in that granite-like wall! I say, Tom, fancy – perhaps we are the very first people to stand in this big underground hall!'

The underground river split into three in the big cavern. One lot of water went downwards into the steep tunnel, one wandered off to the other end of the cavern, and the third entered a smaller tunnel, and ran gently along it as far as Sandy could see.

'We'll follow this second one that goes to the other end of the cave,' said Sandy. 'We needn't wade in it – we can walk beside it. Come on.'

So they walked beside it, and found that it wandered through a narrow archway into yet another cave – and there they saw a strange sight.

The water stopped there and formed a great underground lake, whose waters gleamed purple, green and blue by the light of the boys' torches. The lake was moved by quiet ripples. Tom and Sandy stood gazing at it.

'Isn't it marvellous?' whispered Tom, and

again his whisper ran all round and came back to him in dozens of echoes.

Sandy suddenly got out the candle and lit it. The flame flickered violently and almost went out.

'The air's bad in this cave!' cried Sandy. 'Come back to the other, where the rushing water is! Quick!'

He and Tom left the strange lake, and ran back to the great, shining hall. The air felt much purer at once and the boys took big breaths of it. The candle now burnt steadily.

'For some reason the air isn't good yonder,' said Sandy. 'Well, we can't go *that* way! There's only one way left – and that's to wade down that tunnel over there. Maybe it's the right one!'

'We'll hope so,' said Tom, doing some more exercises, and jumping up and down. 'Come on, Sandy. In we go!'

So into the water they went once more. How cold it was again! The tunnel was quite high above the water, and the stream itself was shallow, only up to their knees. It was quite easy to get along.

They waded along for a long way, their torches lighting up the tunnel. And then a very surprising thing happened.

They heard the murmur of voices! Tom and Sandy listened in the greatest astonishment.

Perhaps it was the noise of the stream? Or strange echoes?

They went on again, and came out into a small cave through which the stream flowed quite placidly. And there they heard the voices again!

Then suddenly the voices stopped, and an even more peculiar sound came. It was the sound of somebody playing an organ!

CHAPTER 10

A VERY STRANGE DISCOVERY

Sandy clutched hold of Tom, for the sound crept into every corner of the cave, and filled it full. They were drowned in music!

It went on and on and then stopped. No further noise came, either of voices or music. The boys flashed their torches into each other's faces and looked at one another in amazement.

'An organ! In the heart of the mountain!' said Tom, in an amazed whisper. 'Didn't it sound wonderful?'

'Come on – let's get out of this cave and see what's in the next one!' whispered Sandy. 'Maybe there's an underground church here, with somebody playing the organ!'

The boys crept along, one behind the other. They suddenly saw a light shining through a rugged opening in the cave. It came from a cave beyond. Sandy peeped round to see what it was.

A lantern swung from a rope in the roof of a cave. It was a large cave, and in it were the two men who lived in the old cottage! They were crouched over the machinery that Sandy had seen in the back room!

Sandy clutched Tom's hand, and his heart leapt and beat fast. So they had actually come to the cave behind the gushing spring that fell from the hole in the rock!

They could hardly believe their good luck! They squeezed each other's hand, and wished that the men would go away from the machinery, whatever it was, so that they might see what it was.

'I wish they'd go back to the cottage,' whispered Sandy – and at once his whisper ran round and round and sounded like a lot of snakes hissing! The men looked up in alarm.

'What was that noise?' said one.

The second man answered in a language that Sandy knew was German. He wasn't deaf and dumb then! Sandy rejoiced. They *were* spies, he felt quite sure. But how could he make them go away, so that he and Tom could examine the cave properly.

Sandy had an idea. He suddenly began to make the most dreadful moaning noises imaginable, like a dog in pain. He made Tom jump – but the two men jumped even more. They sprang up and looked round fearfully.

'Oooh, ah, ooh-ooh-ah, wee-oo, wee-oo, waaaah!' wailed Sandy. The echoes sent the groaning noise round and round the cave, gathering together and becoming louder and louder till the whole place was full of the wildest moaning and wailing you could imagine!

The men shouted something in fear. They ran to the stream, jumped into it, waded in the water till they got to the rock through which it flowed, and then wriggled out of the hole, down to the ground below, on the sunny hillside. They had never in their lives been so terrified.

Tom and Sandy screamed with laughter. They held on to one another, and laughed till they could laugh no more. And the echoes of their laughter ran all around them till it seemed as if the whole place must be full of laughing imps.

'Come on – let's have a look round now,' said Sandy at last. They ran into the men's cave – and then Tom saw what the 'machinery' was!

'It's a radio transmitter!' he cried. 'I've seen one before. These men can send out radio messages as well as receive them – and oh, Sandy, that's what they've been doing, the wretches! As soon as they see the steamers pass on the sea in the distance, they send a radio message to some submarine lurking near by, and the submarine torpedoes the steamers!'

'Oh! So that's why there have been so many steamers sunk round our coast,' said Sandy, his eyes flashing in anger. 'The hateful scoundrels! I'm going to smash their set, anyway!'

Before Tom could stop Sandy, the raging boy picked up a stone and smashed it into the centre of the transmitter. 'You won't sink any *more* steamers!' he cried.

'Good,' said Tom. 'Now let's wriggle to the hole where the stream gushes out, Sandy, and see if the men are anywhere near. If they're not, we could wriggle out, and go back to the girls over-ground. I really don't fancy going all the way back underground!'

'Nor do I,' said Sandy. 'It would be much quicker if we got out here, went up to the top of the mountain, and climbed down from there to where the girls are waiting.'

'Fancy, Sandy – we've been right through the mountain!' said Tom. 'I guess no boy has ever had such an adventure as we've had before!'

'Come on,' said Sandy. 'I'll go first.'

He was soon at the mouth of the hole. He peered out – but there was no one about at all, not even the big dog. 'I bet the men have run into the cottage, taken the dog to guard them, and locked the door!' called back Sandy.

'Well, your wails and groans were enough to

make anyone jump out of their skin!' said Tom. 'I got an awful scare myself, Sandy!'

The two boys wriggled out of the hole, soaked again by the rushing water. But once they stood in the warm sun they forgot their shivers and danced for glee.

'Come on!' said Sandy. 'No time to lose! The climb will make us as warm as can be!'

Off they went, climbing up the mountain-side, revelling in the feel of the warm heather. The sun shone down and very soon they were as warm as toast – too warm, in fact, for Tom began to puff and pant like an engine!

They went over the top at last, sparing a moment to look back at the magnificent view. Far away they could see the blue sea, with a small steamer on it. 'The submarine can't be told about *you*!' said Sandy. 'Come on, Tom.'

On they went. Tom followed Sandy, for Sandy knew every inch of the way. Down the other side they went, scrambling in their swim-suits over the heather. And presently in the distance, they saw the blue frocks of the two girls.

Sheila was bending anxiously over the pot-hole, wishing the boys would come back. It was so long now since they had gone down the hole. She almost fell down it herself when she heard Sandy's shout behind her.

'Hello! Here we are!'

The girls leapt to their feet and looked round in amazement. They were so surprised that they couldn't say a word. Then Jeanie spoke.

'How *did* you get out of the pot-hole?' she gasped. 'Sheila and I have been sitting here for hours, watching – and now you suddenly appear!'

'It's a long story,' said Sandy, 'but a very surprising one. Listen!'

He sat down on the heather and he and Tom told how they had made their way through the heart of the mountain, wading and swimming in the river, and how they had found the strange underground lake, and had taken the right turning to the cave behind the spring. When they told about the men, and how Sandy had frightened them with his groans and wails, the girls flung themselves backwards and squealed with laughter.

'And now we know the secret of why our steamers on this coast are so easily sunk,' finished Sandy. 'It's because of those two traitors and their radio. Well, I smashed that! And now the best thing we can do is to go back home and get the police again!'

'What about our clothes?' asked Tom.

'They can wait,' said Sandy. 'We'll get them from the pot-hole sometime. We ought to go and get the police before the men discover that I've broken their radio, and escape!'

'Come on then!' cried the girls, jumping up, 'We're ready!'

And down the hillside they all tore, the two boys in their swim-suits, with their oil-skin bags still hanging round their necks!

CHAPTER 11

THE HUNT FOR
THE TWO SPIES

Miss Mitchell jumped in surprise when the four children rushed into the garden where she was busy cutting flowers – the boys in their swim-suits, and the girls squealing with excitement.

'Miss Mitchell! Miss Mitchell! We've found out all about the two spies!'

'Miss Mitchell! We've been down the pot-hole!'

'Miss Mitchell! We know how those steamers were sunk!'

'Miss Mitchell! Can we phone the police? Listen, do listen!'

So Miss Mitchell listened, and could hardly believe her ears when the children told her such an extraordinary tale.

'You dared to go down that pot-hole!' she gasped. 'Oh, you naughty, plucky boys! Oh, I can't believe all this, I really can't.'

Mrs MacLaren came home at that moment, and the children streamed to meet her, shouting their news. Mrs MacLaren went pale when she heard how Sandy and Tom had actually climbed down the dangerous pot-hole.

'Well, you certainly won't do *that* again!' she said firmly. 'You might have killed yourselves!'

'But, Mother, our clothes are still down there,' said Sandy. 'We'll have to get them.'

'You are far more important to me than your clothes,' said Mrs MacLaren. 'On no account are you to go pot-hole climbing again! And now – I think I must certainly ring up the police.'

The children clustered round the phone whilst Mrs MacLaren rang the police station. They were so excited that they couldn't keep still!

'Do sit down,' begged Miss Mitchell. 'How *can* your mother phone when you are jigging about like grasshoppers!'

Mrs MacLaren, told the sergeant what the children had discovered. When the sergeant heard that Sandy had smashed the spies' radio with a stone, he roared with laughter.

'Ah, he's a bonny lad, yon boy of yours!' he said into the phone. 'He didn't wait for us to see if that radio was really doing bad work – he smashed it himself! Well, Mrs MacLaren, I'm fine and obliged to your children for doing such good work for us. This is a serious matter, and I must get on to our headquarters now, and take my orders. I'll be along at Kidillin House in a wee while!'

Mrs MacLaren put the phone down and turned to tell the children. 'Can we go with the police, Mother? Oh do let us!' begged Sandy. 'After all, we did find out everything ourselves. And if those men have escaped, by any chance, we would have to show the police how to squeeze in through the rock where the spring gushes out.'

'Very well,' said Mrs MacLaren. 'But go and put some clothes on quickly, and then come down and eat something. You must be very hungry after all these adventures.'

'Well, so I am!' said Jeanie, in surprise. 'But I was so excited that I didn't think of it till you spoke about it, Mother.'

'I'm jolly hungry too, Aunt Jessie!' said Tom. 'Come on, Sandy, let's put on shorts and jerseys, then we'll have time for something to eat before the police come.'

The children expected to see only the constable and the sergeant — and they were immensely sur-prised when a large black car roared up the drive to Kidillin House, with *six* policemen inside!

'Good old police!' said Sheila, watching the men jump out of the car. 'I love our London policemen, they're so tall and kind — but these police look even taller and stronger! I guess they won't stand any nonsense from the spies!'

An inspector was with the police – a stern-looking man, with the sharpest eyes Sandy had ever seen. He beckoned to Sandy and the boy went to him proudly.

'These spies may know they have been discovered, isn't that so?' asked the policeman. 'They have only to go into their cave to see their radio smashed, and they would know that someone had guessed their secret.'

'Yes, sir,' said Sandy. 'So I suggest that half your men go in the car to the other side of the mountain, and go up the slope there – it's a pretty rough road, but the car will do it all right – and the other half come with us up *this* side. Then if the spies try to escape the other way, they will be caught.'

'Good idea,' said the inspector. He gave some sharp orders, and three of the men got into the car and roared away again. When they came to the village of Kidillin, they would take the road that led around the foot of the mountain and would then go up the other side.

'Come on,' said the inspector, and he and the children and two policemen went up the hillside. The dogs, of course, went too, madly excited. Sandy said he could quiet them at any moment, and to show that he could, he held up his finger and called 'Quiet!' At once the two dogs stopped their yelping and lay down flat. The inspector nodded.

'All right,' he said. 'Come along.'

They trooped up the mountainside. When they came fairly near the old cottage, the children had a great disappointment. The inspector forbade them to come any further!'

'These men may be dangerous,' he said. 'You will stay here till I say you may move.'

'But, please, sir,' began Sandy.

'Obey orders!' said the inspector, in a sharp voice. The children stood where they were at once, and the three men went on. The dogs stood quietly by Sandy.

It seemed ages before the children heard anything more. Then they saw one of the policemen coming down the heather towards them.

'The men are gone!' he said. 'Our men the other side didn't meet them, and we've seen no sign of them. Either they've escaped us, or they're hiding somewhere on the hill. They've left their dog though. We've captured it, and it's tied to a tree. Don't let your two go near it.'

The children looked at one another in dismay and disappointment. 'So they've escaped after all!' said Tom. 'Well, what about us showing you where their radio is? We might as well do that whilst we're here.'

So the two boys took the six policemen to the hole in the rock, where the water gushed out. Two of the men squeezed through after Sandy and Tom, who once more got soaked! But they didn't care! Adventures like this didn't happen every day!

The men looked in amazement at the 'machinery' in the cave. 'What a wonderful set,' said one of the policemen, who knew all about radios. 'My word! No wonder we've had our steamers sunk here – these spies had only to watch them passing and send a radio message to the waiting submarine. We'll catch that submarine soon, or my name isn't Jock!'

'It's a strange sort of place, this,' said the other policeman, looking round.

Sandy startled the policeman very much by suddenly clutching his arm and saying 'Sh!'

'Don't do that!' said the man, scared. 'What's up?'

'I heard something over yonder,' said Sandy, pointing to the back of the cave. 'I say – I believe the spies are hiding in the mountain itself! I'm sure I heard a voice back there!'

The policeman whistled. 'Why didn't we think of that before! Come on, then – we'll hunt them out. Do you know the way?'

'Yes,' said Sandy. 'There's another cave behind this, and then a tunnel through which a shallow stream runs, and then a great underground hall, with an odd lake shining in a separate cavern.'

'Good gracious!' said the policeman, staring at Sandy in surprise. 'Well, come on, there's no time to lose.'

They followed Sandy into the next cave. The boy lighted the way with his torch. Then they all waded up the stream in the dark rocky tunnel, and came out into the enormous underground hall.

And at the other end of the great cavern they heard the sound of footfalls, as the two spies groped about, using a torch that was almost finished.

'Give yourselves up!' shouted the first policeman, and his voice echoed round thunderously. The spies put out their light and ran, stumbling and scrambling, into the cave where the underground lake shone mysteriously. Sandy remembered that the air was bad there.

He told the policeman. They put on their own torches and groped their way to the cave of the lake. The air was so bad there that the two spies, after breathing it for a minute or two, had fallen to the ground, quite stupefied.

The policemen tied handkerchiefs round their mouths and noses, and ran in. In a moment they had dragged the two men out of the lake-cave

and whilst they were still drowsy, had quickly handcuffed them. Now they could not escape!

Sandy and Tom were dancing about in excitement. The spies were caught! Their radio was smashed! Things were too marvellous for words!

It took them some time to squeeze out of the hole in the rock, with two handcuffed men, but at last they were all out. The surprise on the inspector's face outside was comical to see!

'They were in there, sir,' said a policeman, jerking his head towards the caves. 'My word, sir, you should see inside that mountain! It's a marvellous place.'

But the inspector was more interested in the capture of the spies. Each of them was handcuffed to a policeman, and down the hill they all came, policemen, spies, children – and dogs! The big dog belonging to the men was taken over the hill by one policeman, to the car left on the road below. Mack and Paddy had barked that they would eat him up, and looked as if they would too!

'So the spy-dog had better go by car!' said the inspector, smiling for the first time.

CHAPTER 12

THE END OF THE
ADVENTURE

What an exciting evening the children had, telling their mother and Miss Mitchell all that had happened! Captain MacLaren came too, on twenty-four hour's leave, for the police had phoned to him, and he felt he must go and hear what had happened.

'It's a great thing, you know, catching those two spies,' he said. 'It means we'll probably get the submarine out there that's been damaging our shipping – for we'll send out a false message, and ask it to get in a certain position to sink a ship – but our aeroplanes will be there to sink the submarine instead!'

'Could we explore the inside of the mountain again, please, Uncle?' asked Tom.

'Not unless I am with you,' said Captain MacLaren firmly. 'I promise you that when I get any good leave, and can come home for two or three weeks, or when the war is over, we'll all go down there exploring together. But you must certainly not explore any more by yourselves. Also, the winter will soon be here, and the rains and snow will swell that underground lake, and the streams, and will fill the caves and tunnels almost to their roofs. It will be too dangerous.'

'Uncle, when we *do* explore the heart of the mountain with you, we could find out if the river there *is* the beginning of the Spelter,' said Tom, eagerly. 'We could throw something into it there – and watch to see if what we throw in, comes out at the foot of the mountain where the river rushes!'

'We could,' said Captain MacLaren, 'and we will! We'll have a wonderful time together, and discover all kinds of strange things!'

'But we shall never have *quite* such an exciting time again, as we've had this last week or two,' said Sandy. 'I couldn't have done it without Tom. I'm jolly glad he and Sheila came to live with us!'

'So am I!' said Tom. 'I'm proud of my Scottish cousins, Uncle Andy!'

'And I'm proud of my English nephew and niece!' said the captain, clapping Tom on the back. He looked at them with a twinkle in his eye. 'I *did* hear that you couldn't bear one another at one time,' he said, 'and that you and the dogs were all fighting together!'

'Yes, that's true,' said Sandy, going red. 'But we're all good friends now. Mack! You like old Paddy, don't you?'

Mack and Paddy were lying down side by side. At Sandy's words Mack sat up, cocked his ears, and then licked Paddy on the nose with his red tongue!

'There you are!' said Sandy, pleased. 'That shows you what good friends they are! But I shan't lick Tom's nose to show he's *my* friend!'

Everybody laughed, and then Miss Mitchell spoke.

'I wonder what's happening to those two spies,' she said. And at that very moment the telephone rang. It was the inspector, who had called up the captain to tell him the latest news.

'One of the men is a famous spy,' he said. 'We've had our eye on him for years, and he disappeared when war broke out. We are thankful to have caught him!'

'I should think so!' said the captain. 'What a bit of luck! It's difficult to round up all these spies – they're so clever at disappearing!'

'Well, sir, they won't do any more disappearing – except into prison!' chuckled the inspector. 'And now there's another bit of news, sir – I don't know if you've heard it?'

'I've heard nothing,' said the captain. 'What's the second piece of news, inspector?'

'It's about that submarine, sir. We've spotted it – and we've damaged it so that it couldn't sink itself properly.'

'Good work!' cried the captain in joy. 'That *is* a fine bit of news!'

'We've captured the submarine,' went on the inspector, 'and we've taken all the crew prisoners.'

'What have you done with the submarine?' asked the captain, whilst all the children crowded round him in excitement, trying to guess all that was said at the other end of the telephone.

'The submarine is being towed to Port Riggy,' said the inspector, 'and if the children would like to come over and see it next week, we'll be very pleased to take them over it, to show them what they've helped to capture!'

'What does he say, what does he say?' cried Sandy. 'Quick, tell us, Father!'

'Oh, he just wants to know if you'd like to go over to Port Riggy next week, and see the submarine you helped to capture!' said the captain, smiling round at the four eager faces.

'Who said we should never have such an exciting time as we've been having!' yelled Tom, dancing round like a clumsy bear. 'Golly! Think of going over a submarine! Miss Mitchell – you'll have to give us a day's holiday next week, won't you!'

'Oh, it depends on how hard you work,' said Miss Mitchell, with a wicked twinkle in her eye.

And my goodness, how hard those four children are working now! They couldn't possibly miss going over to Port Riggy to see that submarine, could they?

WIN A WEEKEND BREAK
FOR YOUR FAMILY AT CENTER PARCS

THE COMPETITION WILL BE JUDGED BY ENID BLYTON'S DAUGHTER,
GILLIAN BAVERSTOCK, AND THE FIVE LUCKY WINNERS WILL BE
ANNOUNCED ON THE 19TH AUGUST 1997.

HOW TO ENTER

1. Solve the riddle:

   My first is in apple and also in pear
   My second's in rabbit but never in hare
   My third is in lucky but not in thirteen
   My fourth is in runner and also in bean
   My fifth is in tortoise and also in snail
   My last is in bucket but never in pail
   My whole is a pleasure to go on together
   But better watch out for the wasps and the weather!

   _____

2. Now describe the most amazing adventure you've ever had
   (using no more than 30 words):

   _____
   _____
   _____
   _____
   _____
   _____

Please send your entries on this form to the following address:
Blyton/Center Parcs Competition
Bloomsbury Publishing Plc, 38 Soho Square, London W1V 5DF.

Name: _____ Age: _____

Address: _____

_____

Telephone Number: _____

Signature of a parent/responsible adult: _____

The competition is open to any child of twelve years and under and resident in the U.K.
All entries must be signed by a parent or guardian.
See overleaf for Terms and Conditions.

CLOSING DATE FOR ENTRIES: 31ST JULY 1997.

Terms and Conditions

1. Bloomsbury Publishing Plc cannot take any responsibility for the return of any entries to the competition.

2. The competition is open to any child of twelve years and under and resident in the U.K, subject to signature of parent or guardian. No employees of Bloomsbury Publishing Plc, Center Parcs or their agents are eligible to enter the competition.

3. The prizes for winning entries will be the ones specified only. They may not be changed and are non-transferable. No substitute prizes or cash alternatives are available. The prizes consist of the use of a 3-bedroom villa for a family of up to 6 at a UK Center Parcs Village, plus £150 worth of Center Parcs' vouchers which can be spent in the Village. It does not include any additional charges such as meals, insurance, sports & leisure activities or other personal expenses. Travel expenses are covered up to the value of £50 per prize. Bookings are subject to availability and to the terms and conditions published in Center Parcs' brochure.
The prizes should be taken by Spring 1998.

4. All entries must be received by 31st July1997. All entries must be submitted using this competition page, photocopies will not be accepted. Incomplete, illegible, spoilt or late entries will not be considered.

5. The prizes will be awarded to the entrants who have correctly solved the riddle and, in the judge's opinion, have submitted the most apt, original and amazing adventure. All entries will be judged by Gillian Baverstock. Her decision is final and no correspondence will be entered into.

6. Winners will be notified by post or telephone, no later than Monday 11th August. The winners will be required to attend a party on 19th August 1997 to announce the prizes to the press, they may also be required to attend picture-taking for publicity purposes without compensation, other than reasonable out of pocket expenses.

7. Details of winners and results will be available by post after 11th August. If required please send a stamped, self-addressed envelope to Blyton/Center Parcs Competition, Bloomsbury Publishing Plc, 38 Soho Square, London, W1V 5DF.

8. All entry instructions form part of the rules and the submission of an entry will be deemed to signify acceptance of these rules by the entrant. Closing date for entries 31st July 1997.

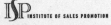

INSTITUTE OF SALES PROMOTION

ISP Registration Number: 658
Rules conform to the Institute of Sales Promotion recommended practice.